Who's Hiding?

Agnese Baruzzi

little bee books

The veggie patch conceals a beast
who's munching up a carrot feast!

With a cotton tail and furry ears,
which creature's found its dinner here?

Some rustling leaves! Is it the breeze?
Or is there something in the trees?

Which creature has begun to stir,
with antlers, hooves, and soft, brown fur?

In the pond one creature swims,
stretching out its long green limbs.

Who croaks and leaps and hops like mad
and perches on a lily pad?

In the garden's shady cool
grow many kinds of bright toadstool.

Which spotted creature's hiding here
whose shell can make it disappear?

Among the palms, two creatures dance.
They twist and flutter, bob and prance.

With feathered wings and pointed beak;
who goes there? Take a peek!

Some thorny flowers in the grass
bend to let a creature pass.

Green and scaly, quick and sly—
who tries to catch a butterfly?

Feathery, furry, big and small.
Hoppy, spotty, short and tall.

How many creatures can you name,
playing their favorite hiding game?